MAURICE the UNBEASTLY

Amy Dixon

illustrated by Karl James Mountford

STERLING CHILDREN'S BOOKS
New York

MAURICE was not like the other Beasts.

His voice was as sweet and refreshing
as dandelion lemonade on a hot day.

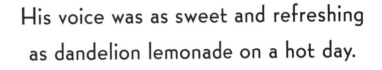

He preferred
his snacks green

and organic.

And he was
ridiculously photogenic.

Mama and Papa Beast
were concerned.

"Beasts
ROAR!"
said Mama.

"And
DESTROY!"
bellowed Papa.

"You must learn to be less civilized," Mama said. "We are enrolling you at the Abominable Academy for Brutish Beasts."

Maurice munched quietly on his
kale kabob and mulled this over.
He was a Beast. He was supposed to
be fierce and ugly and gruff. He didn't
want to be a gargantuan failure.

So he tidied up his room, packed up his alfalfa fritters, and headed off to the Abominable Academy for Brutish Beasts.

THE ABOMINABLE ACADEMY

FOR BRUTISH BEASTS

HEAR US ROAR
HIT THE FLOOR
WE'RE THE MIGHTY
CARNIVORE!

"Our first lesson," growled the Headmaster, "will be the frightening ROAR!"

The Beasts responded in a chorus of terrifying shouts—except for Maurice, whose voice rose above the rest in a perfect high A.

ToDay's LESSON THE ROAR!

A note went home to Mama and Papa:
"Maurice's roar is dreadfully melodious
and delightful to the ear."

"Lesson number two,"
the Headmaster snarled,
"is MESSY meat eating!"

The Beasts ripped and ravaged through the
meat feast before them—except for Maurice,
who placed a napkin in his lap and said, "Excuse me,
please, but is there a vegetarian option?"

Another note went home to Mama and Papa:
"Maurice is terribly neat and polite.
And we had to confiscate
his alfalfa fritters."

"Next," said the Headmaster,
"we DESTROY!"

Each Beast in the room crashed and
crushed, wrecked and ruined—

except for Maurice,
who dashingly dodged

and stylishly side-stepped
the mayhem.

"You're much too light
on your feet!" the
Headmaster scolded.

Just when Maurice thought
it couldn't get any worse,
picture day arrived.

One by one, the Beasts
thundered through the line,
their hideousness shattering
camera lenses.

Maurice was determined
to get this one right.

He growled and scowled.
He snarled and howled.

The photographer still captured
the perfect glamour shot.

One last note went home:
"If Maurice insists on continuing to
smile, he will never progress."

Maurice was beginning to feel as if
the Abominable Academy for Brutish
Beasts was a gargantuan mistake.

Just then, a ruckus erupted
in the classroom.

An unidentified creature
had infiltrated the academy.

One Beast roared, but the
creature just roared right back.

Another Beast bravely tried to catch it,
but she stomped much too slowly.

All the Beasts quivered
and quaked . . .

. . . except for Maurice, who sashayed
to the left and flashed his winning smile.
"Here, creature-creature," he sang.

The creature stopped and
looked with big eyes at Maurice.

Maurice pulled a hidden
alfalfa fritter from his
pocket and held it out.

The other Beasts watched in amazement as the creature bounded over to Maurice and curled up in his lap.

"Teach us this creature magic!" the Headmaster said.

And so Maurice was named The Official Creature
Whisperer of the Abominable Academy for Brutish Beasts.

He was a gargantuan success.

His paper, "Coaxing Creatures 101: Using the Beast's Softer Side," won first prize in the school essay contest.

He led a campaign to add kale to the lunch menu.

And he started the academy's first a cappella group, The Barbaritones.

Maurice was definitely not like the other Beasts.

And thank goodness for that.

The End

STERLING CHILDREN'S BOOKS
New York

An Imprint of Sterling Publishing Co., Inc.
1166 Avenue of the Americas
New York, NY 10036

Text © 2017 by Amy Dixon
Illustrations © 2017 by Karl J. Mountford

ISBN 978-1-4549-1953-7

Library of Congress Cataloging-in-Publication Data

Names: Dixon, Amy, 1975- author. | Mountford, Karl James, illustrator.
Title: Maurice the unbeastly / by Amy Dixon ; illustrated by Karl J. Mountford.
Description: New York : Sterling Children's Books, [2017] | Summary: No ordinary
beast, Maurice is neat, polite, photogenic, and his roar is delightful to the ear, which
leads his parents to enroll him at the Abominable Academy for Brutish Beasts, where
he realizes he has a few things he can teach his fellow beasts.
Identifiers: LCCN 2016033361 | ISBN 9781454919537
Subjects: | CYAC: Monsters—Fiction. | Schools—Fiction. | Individuality—Fiction.
Classification: LCC PZ7.D6417 Mau 2017 | DDC [E]—dc23 LC record available at
https://lccn.loc.gov/2016033361

Distributed in Canada by Sterling Publishing Co., Inc.
c/o Canadian Manda Group, 664 Annette Street
Toronto, Ontario, Canada M6S 2C8
Distributed in the United Kingdom by GMC Distribution Services
Castle Place, 166 High Street, Lewes, East Sussex, England BN7 1XU
Distributed in Australia by NewSouth Books
45 Beach Street, Coogee, NSW 2034, Australia

For information about custom editions, special sales, and premium and corporate purchases,
please contact Sterling Special Sales at 800-805-5489 or specialsales@sterlingpublishing.com.

Manufactured in China

Lot #:
2 4 6 8 10 9 7 5 3 1
06/17

www.sterlingpublishing.com

The artwork for this book was created using traditional and digital mixed media . . .
and the occasional roar of an untamed artist.
Design by Ryan Thomann